GREEN THUMBS-UP!

Read the second book in the

FRIENDSHIP GARDEN

series:

Pumpkin Spice

the FRIENDSHIP garden

GREEN THUMBS-UP!

by Jenny Meyerhoff
illustrated by Éva Chatelain

ALADDIN
New York London Toronto Sydney New Delhi

ALADDIN

An imprint of Simon & Schuster Children's Publishing Division

1230 Avenue of the Americas, New York, NY 10020

This Aladdin paperback edition August 2015

Text copyright © 2015 by Simon & Schuster, Inc.

Illustrations copyright © 2015 by Éva Chatelain

Also available in an Aladdin hardcover edition.

All rights reserved, including the right of reproduction in whole or in part in any form.

ALADDIN is a trademark of Simon & Schuster, Inc., and related logo is a registered trademark of Simon & Schuster, Inc.

For information about special discounts for bulk purchases, please contact Simon & Schuster Special Sales at 1-866-506-1949 or business@simonandschuster.com.

The Simon & Schuster Speakers Bureau can bring authors to your live event. For more information or to book an event contact the Simon & Schuster Speakers Bureau at 1-866-248-3049 or visit our website at www.simonspeakers.com.

Book designed by Laura Lyn DiSiena

The text of this book was set in Century Expanded LT Std.

Manufactured in the United States of America 0715 OFF

10 9 8 7 6 5 4 3 2 1

Library of Congress Cataloging-in-Publication Data

Meyerhoff, Jenny.

Green thumbs-up! / by Jenny Meyerhoff ; illustrated by Éva Chatelain. — First Aladdin paperback edition.

p. cm. — (The friendship garden ; 1)

Summary: Third grader Anna has had trouble making friends since her family moved from a small town in New York to Chicago, but a group project at school leads to new opportunities, including friendships, a club, and a garden she can work in, just like in her last home.

[1. Friendship—Fiction. 2. Gardening—Fiction. 3. Clubs—Fiction. 4. Schools—Fiction. 5. Moving, Household—Fiction. 6. Family life—Illinois—Chicago—Fiction. 7. Chicago (Ill.)—Fiction.] I. Chatelain, Éva, illustrator. II. Title.

PZ7.M571753Gre 2015 [Fic]—dc23 2014045750

ISBN 978-1-4814-3906-0 (hc)

ISBN 978-1-4814-3904-6 (pbk)

ISBN 978-1-4814-3907-7 (eBook)

For Helen and Jim, who helped
Chicago feel like home

CONTENTS

CHAPTER 1

CHICAGO BLUES

G-R-A-Y.

That's what Anna saw when she looked out the window of her third-grade classroom at Sullivan Magnet School. Gray sky. Gray playground. Gray sidewalk. Even the squirrels were gray. All that gray made Anna's brain bleary. Ever since she'd moved to Chicago last week, Anna *felt* gray.

At her old school in New York—not New York City, like everyone seemed to think when they heard "New York," but a tiny town called Rosendale—the view from Anna's classroom was bursting with green. But through the window at Anna's school in downtown Chicago, the only hint of color was the orange safety vest of the playground monitor.

Her teacher, Mr. Hoffman, stood at the smart board. He pushed his clicker and words appeared on the screen. *Persuasive Speech.*

"In a *persuasive* speech you must persuade someone; that is, convince them to do or believe something. This week you will work in small groups to write and present a persuasive speech to our class."

Anna glanced around the room. The phrase "small groups" sent a tingle of worry up her

spine. Although the other students were looking around too, no one looked Anna's way. Who could she work with?

It was only the fourth day of school and Anna hadn't made any friends yet. Her parents kept telling her that she was just "between" friends, but that was hard to believe, especially since none of her new classmates would even look at her.

A few kids at school seemed like they might be okay, but others made it clear that they weren't looking for new friends. These were mostly girls who dressed like movie stars and carried cell phones everywhere. In her head, Anna had nicknamed those girls the Outfit-Outfit, since *outfit* was another word for a group, and *this* outfit seemed to care a lot about their outfits. Anna liked nicknaming things.

"You may choose any topic," Mr. Hoffman continued, "as long as everyone in your group agrees."

If Hayley and Lauren were in Anna's classroom, the three of them wouldn't even have to ask if they wanted to work together. They just knew those kinds of things by looking at one another. Back in Rosendale, they had done everything together. Anna had named their group the True-Blue Besties.

Over by the big glass aquarium sat a girl with dark wavy hair and glasses who was always first to raise her hand when Mr. Hoffman asked a question. Her name was Kaya. Anna had noticed that Kaya took turns writing with a different colored pencil for every subject. Anna thought she might ask Kaya to work with her, but she didn't know if she could persuade Kaya to say yes. First she'd have to persuade Kaya to put down her colored pencils. Whenever Kaya wasn't doing schoolwork, she was drawing.

Anna was pretty sure she wasn't any good at persuading. She had tried to persuade her parents not to move to Chicago, but they moved anyway.

Mr. Hoffman straightened his bow tie. Every day he wore blue jeans, a button-down shirt, and a bow tie. He straightened his bow tie a lot. Anna wondered if it was too tight.

Every day Anna wore tights or socks with an interesting pattern. Today she wore rainbow-striped kneesocks. At her old school, her classmates were always interested in what tights Anna was wearing. At her new school, no one ever noticed them. Except for the Outfit-Outfit. On the first day of school, the leader of the Outfit-Outfit, Mackenzie, had said, "What's on your tights? Pictures of *beetles*?" It had actually been pictures of seven-spot ladybirds, which *are* a kind of beetle, but Anna decided not to tell Mackenzie that.

"*I* will assign the groups," Mr. Hoffman announced, and Anna breathed a sigh of relief. The Outfit-Outfit groaned.

Mr. Hoffman continued. "Right now you will have fifteen minutes to talk about your ideas. Speeches will be given on Friday, so you have five days to complete the assignment."

Anna's eyes searched the room again.

Jessica, a girl with red curly hair and braces, didn't look at her. Reed, a boy with reddish hair and colorful, squeezy, squishy stress balls on his desk, didn't look at her. Neither did Sarah and Mona, the twins with glasses.

"Group number one," said Mr. Hoffman. "Anna Fincher."

Anna crossed her fingers.

"Kaya Reynolds," continued Mr. Hoffman. Kaya put down her pencil and looked at Anna. Anna smiled. Kaya straightened her glasses, picked up a different pencil, and started to sketch.

"Reed Madigan." Mr. Hoffman pointed to the far corner of the room. "Group One can meet near the book nook. Bring pencils and notebooks."

Anna grabbed her things and met Kaya

and Reed in the book nook. Reed brought his orange squeezy ball.

Squeeze. Squeeze.

Anna sat cross-legged on the rug of the United States map. She decided to sit right on top of New York. Maybe her old state would bring her luck. "What should our speech be about?" she asked.

Kaya opened her notebook and wrote *Persuasive Speech* at the top in purple pencil. "We should persuade everyone, including my parents, that all kids need pets," Kaya suggested. Then she drew a picture of a dog.

"Everyone knows that!" Reed squeezed the orange ball double-time. "I think we should persuade everyone that recess should last three hours every day."

"I don't think it will be hard to convince *kids*, but I doubt we could convince Mr. Hoffman." Kaya wrote Reed's idea under her own, but she doodled a green and yellow question mark next to it.

Anna thought she might have an idea. She wasn't sure if she should say it out loud. It wasn't the best idea she'd ever had. Anna figured she'd need a really good idea if she was going to make new friends.

"Do you have any ideas?" Kaya asked Anna, her purple pencil now poised over her notebook.

Anna shook her head. She decided to wait until she had a better idea.

"We all have to agree," Reed reminded them.

Kaya nodded and chewed on the tip of

her pencil. "Let's go home and think of three topics each. Tomorrow we can go to my place after school and pick one."

Reed pulled another squeezy ball out of his pocket. A green one. He squeezed the balls in alternating patterns. *Green. Orange. Green. Orange.* "Sounds good to me."

Anna nodded. "Me too."

She tried to act like it was no big deal, but inside she was jumping for joy. This would be her first time going to somebody else's house since arriving in Chicago.

Butterflies fluttered in her stomach. Not real ones, of course, but the imaginary ones that seemed to pop up whenever Anna felt nervous. Since Anna had moved, butterflies seemed to be showing up in her stomach a lot.

Anna looked at the floor. She looked at Kaya.

"Don't forget," Kaya reminded them as she drew a swirly, curly blue number three in her notebook. "Three ideas."

CHAPTER 2

IT'S NOT EASY FEELING GREEN

After school Anna met her father by the front doors. He carried a big umbrella because it had started to drizzle. From the outside, Mr. Fincher's umbrella was black, but when you stood underneath it, the inside of the umbrella looked like a clear blue sky with puffy white clouds and a hint of sunshine.

Anna stood next to her father under their

private sunny sky. All around them, other students walked home in pairs and small groups. In Rosendale, Anna rode the bus home. The True-Blue Besties always sat together. Some weeks Anna played at a different friend's house every day.

In Chicago, Anna played with her younger brother, Collin, every day after school. It wasn't really much fun.

"Anna Banana! How was Writers' Workshop?" Mr. Fincher asked. "How was Makerspace?"

"Okay," said Anna. "And all right."

"Would you like to invite anyone over today?"

Anna's father asked Anna and Collin that question every single day. Today Anna answered the way she always did. "Not yet."

"Maybe tomorrow." Mr. Fincher gave the same response every day. Then he grabbed Anna's hand and started walking down the block, singing, *"Hi-ho, hi-ho, it's home from school we go."* As always, he sang in a deep voice and swung his arms wildly as he walked. When Anna was in the first and second grades, she thought this was hilarious. But now that she was in third grade, she worried that her dad looked goofy. She glanced around, hoping no one from her class saw him.

All of a sudden, Anna stopped. "Wait!" She couldn't believe her father had forgotten. He'd only been a stay-at-home dad for one week. So far he had forgotten to pack a drink in Anna's lunch box and couldn't remember how to braid hair, but how could he forget an entire first grader?

"What about Collin?" she asked. "We can't leave him at school!"

Anna's father gave her hand a reassuring pat. "We aren't leaving him. A boy named Jax invited him over to play this afternoon."

"Oh." A different feeling filled her chest. Her mother called it the green-eyed monster. Anna felt jealous. "I'm glad Collin made a friend," she said, though she wasn't quite sure she felt *all the way* glad. Now she was the only one with no one to play with.

Anna's sneakers squeaked along the wet pavement as she and her father crossed the street and started the six-block walk home. The first block was filled with coffee shops, clothing stores, and people. Lots of people. Even in the rain, Anna's neighborhood was B-U-S-Y.

Her old neighborhood had been Q-U-I-E-T. There were no shops, only houses and lots of trees.

"Don't worry," said Anna's father as they stepped onto the sidewalk. "You'll make a friend soon, just like Mom and I said. Collin did, and so will you!"

Anna nodded. She was sure her father was right. Only, it was easier for first graders like Collin. In first grade everyone was making new friends. By third grade, friendships were set. No one in Anna's class was *looking* for a new friend. But maybe they could bump into friendship by accident.

"I did get invited to someone's house tomorrow after school," Anna told her father. "A girl named Kaya."

"That's great!" her father said.

"It's only for a school project, though."

"That's still great."

They turned the next corner. This block had two restaurants, a beauty shop, and a bunch of small apartment buildings that looked like giant houses with extra front doors.

"Speaking of projects, want to help me with a cooking project this afternoon?" asked Mr. Fincher. "I thought I'd try making lasagna."

Anna looked at her father. "Sure," she said. Then she added, "Mom's lasagna?"

Anna's father nodded slowly. "Yep. Well, almost. I'm going to make a few adjustments of my own."

Anna forced a smile. Truthfully, her dad wasn't the best cook. When they lived in Rosendale, Anna had loved helping her mom in the kitchen. Now Anna's mother had a new job as a chef at a fancy restaurant. Her dad stayed home, and he was in charge of most of the cooking. This involved him making a lot of "adjustments" to her mom's recipes, most of which didn't taste very good.

Anna and her father stopped at a little corner market. The vegetables on the shelves were soft and wrinkly. They looked like they had been sitting there a while, so Anna's father bought cans of tomatoes and spinach, and also some pasta and cheese. Anna's mother used to make lasagna with the tomatoes and vegetables from the Finchers' garden in New York. Anna loved lasagna because each slice looked like a rainbow.

Finally Anna and her father arrived at

their block. There were no more stores, only houses sitting very close together.

Anna and her father unloaded the groceries. Then they started making dinner.

"I'll crack the eggs!" Anna loved the sound of the shell crunching against the edge of the countertop. Today she didn't even get any pieces of shell in the bowl.

"Egg-cellent!" said her father. "Now, where is that can opener?"

Anna, Collin, and their father had unpacked most of their moving boxes, but they didn't always remember where they'd put everything.

"Let's play Two-Minute Treasure Hunt!" That was the game Anna had invented to search for missing items. She liked making up games too. Games and names.

Anna's father set the kitchen timer. "Two minutes. Ready? Set? Go!"

Anna opened drawer after drawer and then cabinet after cabinet. "What's it doing in here?" she asked as she pulled the can opener out of a soup pot.

Mr. Fincher scratched his head. "Maybe I put it there for when I open cans of soup?"

Anna opened all the tomato cans with the can opener and helped spread the ingredients into the pan. When the lasagna was ready to bake, she went to her room.

It was fun to cook with her dad, but it wasn't the same as playing with a friend. Or even playing with her brother.

Anna watered the houseplants she kept in her room. She had three: a fern named

Fern, a spider plant named Chloe, and a cactus named Spike. She sang them a song because she'd seen on TV that talking and singing to plants helped them grow. Then she sat down on her rainbow-striped bedspread. Her bedroom in Chicago looked almost the same as her bedroom in New York. It had all the same things in it, but it didn't feel the same.

Anna pulled out her notebook and a pen. She had to think of three possible topics for her persuasive speech.

1. Everyone should recycle.
2. Bugs are cool, not creepy.
3. You guys should be my friends.

Anna read her list out loud to her plants and wrinkled her nose. Her first idea was

obvious. Her second idea might seem a little weird. And her third idea . . .

"What do you think, Fern?" Anna asked.

Fern thought her third idea was just plain embarrassing.

Anna closed her notebook and headed to the kitchen for dinner. Collin was home and setting the table as Mr. Fincher pulled the lasagna out of the oven. Anna grabbed the laptop and set it at the head of the table. Then she clicked on the link that would connect them with her mom. Anna's mother had to be at the restaurant most nights, but she could always say hello on the computer for a few minutes.

"Hey, guys! What's for dinner?" Mrs. Fincher asked when she was connected.

"Lasagna!" Mr. Fincher held the casserole up to the computer so his wife could see.

"I hope it's as good as yours, Mom." Collin sat down and spread his napkin on his lap.

Mr. Fincher served everyone a steaming square. Anna was just a tiny bit afraid to try it. She didn't want to hurt her dad's feelings, but she also knew that it probably wouldn't taste as good as her mother's.

Still, she closed her eyes, took a bite, and chewed.

Then she opened her eyes and chewed some more. The cheese was gooey and the noodles were springy, but the tomatoes tasted like pennies. Not that Anna tasted pennies very often.

"So . . . how is it?" Mrs. Fincher asked from the computer screen.

"Not *that* bad," said Mr. Fincher, chewing thoughtfully. "For a first try."

"It's gross," said Collin happily. "Did you know that houseflies can taste with their feet? I'm glad I don't have to put my feet on this lasagna!"

Anna took another bite. The lasagna was just like everything else in Chicago. Not completely terrible, but not quite right either.

CHAPTER 3

TWO GREEN THUMBS-UP . . . OR DOWN

The next day, after the last bell rang, Anna walked out of school with Kaya and Reed. She saw her father waiting for Collin and Collin's new friend Jax over by the basketball hoops. She gave her dad a little wave. Mr. Fincher gave her two thumbs-up.

Anna knew they were just going to work

on a school project, but she couldn't help hoping. Maybe today was the day she'd make her first *real* friends.

Reed shouted good-bye to some boys across the playground. Then he asked Kaya, "Where's your nanny?"

Anna wondered if all the kids at Sullivan had nannies. Would they think it was weird that she was picked up by her father?

"I get picked up by my *abuela*." Kaya pointed at the gate. Anna saw a woman with curly red hair, a bright pink jacket, and green rubber boots with little eyes on the front. The boots looked like frogs.

"What's an *abuela*?" Anna asked.

"It's Spanish for grandmother, duh," Reed explained, then turned to Kaya. "But *that's* your grandma? She doesn't look like my grandma."

"I know." Kaya shrugged and led them over to the gate. "Daisy watches me after school while my parents are at work."

"Hi, *niños*!" Kaya's grandmother kissed Kaya on her forehead, leaving a bright pink lipstick smudge, then she reached out and shook hands with Anna. "Everyone calls me Daisy. *Mucho gusto*. It's very nice to meet you. How do you do?" She did a little curtsy. Anna knew that curtsying was something princesses did in stories, but she had never seen a real person do it.

"Daisy," Kaya hissed through clenched teeth. Her cheeks were as pink as Daisy's lipstick. Anna was surprised that Kaya called her grandmother by her first name.

"What?" Daisy waved a hand in the air. "We need a proper introduction."

"I'm Reed Riley Madigan." Reed stretched out his arm and shook hands with Daisy. "It's a pleasure to make your acquaintance. But why doesn't Kaya call you *abuela* or grandma?"

Daisy beamed at Reed. "Now *that's* an introduction. And I told you. *Everyone* calls me Daisy."

Anna thought Reed sounded like an old man. She had no idea how to talk like that. It was kind of cool and kind of weird. Just like Daisy seemed to be.

"I'm Anna," Anna told Daisy. "Nice to meet you."

"You two must be the most polite children at this school, and that's a good thing," Daisy said, her eyes sparkling. "I only like polite children. The other kind? I string them up by their toes!"

"I don't know," said Reed with a big smile. "Maybe I should stop being polite. Hanging by my toes could be fun!"

"This way, *niños*." Daisy turned the opposite way out of the schoolyard from Anna's house. As Anna followed, she wondered why Daisy was wearing rain boots. It wasn't raining today and the puddles from yesterday were all gone.

"That's my parents' shop," Kaya said as they walked past a frozen yogurt store called FroYo Go.

"FroYo? Can we stop?" Reed asked.

Daisy glanced over her shoulder and winked. "No time for stopping. Besides, I have sweet and sour mudballs and chalk chip cookies waiting at home."

"Yum!" Reed crossed his eyes and rubbed his stomach.

Anna was sure Daisy was kidding. "I like fleas and quackers," she said.

"We've got plenty of quackers, but we're fresh out of fleas."

"Ugh. Daisy, now you've got everyone doing it." Kaya rolled her eyes at her grandmother. "Daisy doesn't have a serious bone in her body."

"But I do have a funny bone and a humerus." Daisy chuckled.

She turned the corner and led the three children down a block filled with small apartment buildings.

Daisy stopped in front of a rusty old gate. Anna couldn't see what was behind it because the fence was overgrown with ivy. Anna's old school had been covered in ivy. When no one was looking, she snuck her hand out to touch it. It was waxy and smooth and so G-R-E-E-N!

Above the gate a crooked sign read OMMUNITY GAR EN.

Daisy pushed the gate open and led them into a wide lot bursting with plants of all shapes and sizes. Anna saw every shade of green—from deep, dark forest green to bright yellow-green—and flowers in every

shade of red, purple, yellow, orange, and blue. Her nose filled with a fresh, earthy scent that made her whole body think, *home*.

"Wait here, *niños*. I've got to water." Daisy grabbed a black hose from a stand next to the gate and dragged it to a wooden rectangle. Anna knew the rectangle was called a planting bed. Now Anna noticed that she wasn't standing in the middle of one giant jungle. Each grouping of plants burst out of its own wooden rectangle. All the rectangles were raised off the ground and had narrow paths between them.

At the very back of the lot, in a rectangle much longer and narrower than all the others, was what looked like a plant junkyard. The plants were so tall, and grew in so many directions, they seemed to be trying to escape their space. Some of them were wilted and dying.

"Is this where you live?" Anna whispered to Kaya.

"What's an 'ommunity garen'?" Reed added.

"The sign is supposed to say 'Community Garden,'" Kaya said. "But some of the letters fell off. And we don't live here, our apartment is down the block. But between April and November, it sometimes feels like Daisy lives here. Her garden is the only thing she doesn't joke about. She says she was born with green thumbs and green

big toes, but she keeps those covered with her gardening boots."

Anna's own thumbs twitched with interest at the sound of the word *garden*. Back in New York, her family's garden was H-U-G-E. Last summer her parents had even let the True-Blue Besties have their own small garden patch to grow carrots and cucumbers.

"Do you ever plant anything?" Anna asked Kaya.

Kaya wrinkled her nose. "Only when Daisy makes me!"

"*I* wouldn't mind digging in that dirt." Reed looked longingly at a big pile of soil. "Even if it does smell like dirty diapers."

"Come on, you guys!" Kaya said. "We

really need to work on our speech, not mess around in a stinky garden."

Anna knew Kaya was right; they did have to get to work. But they would never accidentally become friends if *all* they did was work.

CHAPTER 4

ANNA PICKED A PURPLE PEPPER

"Who's here?" A voice called out of nowhere, making Anna jump.

Anna looked around, but all she could see was a little shed in the front corner of the lot. It looked like a teeny-tiny barn, painted red with a black door and white trim.

A smiling woman poked her head out of the shed. She had brown curly hair that stuck out in all directions. "Kaya!" she said. "Good to see you again! Should we give your friends the grand tour?"

Kaya didn't look like she wanted a tour, but the woman continued without waiting for an answer. "Welcome to the Shoots and Leaves Community Garden. I'm Maria, garden president."

"President?" Anna asked. "We had a garden at my old house, but it didn't need a president."

"In the city, most of us don't have enough space to have a garden of our own. So we converted this empty area into a garden for neighbors to share. Each of these wooden rectangles can be rented out for growing vegetables, flowers, or both. Tell your parents! The garden is always looking for new members."

"What about that?" Reed said, tilting his head toward the overgrown area at the back— the plant junkyard. "That doesn't look like a garden. It looks more like a rotting jungle."

Anna didn't want to say so, but she agreed. Maria looked like she agreed too.

"That plot belongs to the Dupree family. I'm sorry to say it, but they aren't taking very good care of their garden. No one has stopped by in months, and now it's filled with rotting vegetables. It's starting to attract flies and raccoons. I'm worried their weeds are going to take over *everyone's* gardens."

"How can weeds take over?" Kaya asked. "They don't walk around like animals."

"Maybe they're zombies!" Reed stuck his arms out and waddled back and forth. "I am a zombie weed. I need cucumber brains."

Anna and Kaya laughed, but Maria looked serious. "Weeds are no joke," she said. "If they live long enough, they make seeds, like every other plant. But weeds are really good at spreading their seeds around, by wind or by animal. Before you know it their seeds are all over the garden and new weeds start sprouting everywhere."

Anna looked at the plant junkyard. Even if it was messy, it still gave her the peaceful feeling she got whenever she saw something green and growing.

Daisy put the hose back and gave Maria a big hug hello. "Did you get the broccoli seedlings yet? I'll have to plant them soon so that I can harvest broccoli before the first frost."

Maria nodded and tilted her head back

toward the shed. "They just arrived this morning. You can plant them right now if you like. Good thing you brought helpers."

Daisy smiled at Anna, Kaya, and Reed. She raised her eyebrows.

Kaya shook her head. "No way. We have to work on a project for school."

Anna sighed as quietly as she could. Everywhere she went in her new city she saw sidewalks and buildings and even some trees, but nothing as colorful and alive as this garden. She wanted to sit still and breathe the colors in. It was so much like her old garden in New York.

"We could talk about our project while we plant," Anna suggested.

"Will we still get snacks?" Reed asked.

"Did someone say snacks?" Maria ducked

back into her little shed, then came out again carrying a tray full of green, red, yellow, and purple bell pepper slices. These didn't look anything like the sad-looking vegetables Anna had seen at the corner market with her dad.

"I just picked the last of my peppers," Maria said. "Taste."

Reed looked doubtful. "I hate vegetables." Then his face brightened. "But I like snacks." He grabbed a handful and dug in. His expression grew brighter as he crunched. "Mmm. Not bad."

Kaya tried some red pepper slices. Anna stared at the platter for a moment. It reminded  her of a rainbow. Rainbow was Anna's favorite color. She took a bite of purple pepper and let the crisp, juicy sweetness fill her mouth.

After they finished eating, Maria handed the three of them tools that Anna knew were called trowels. They looked like tiny shovels. Daisy also handed each of them trays of plants in little plastic pots.

"We need to dig holes that are three inches deep and three inches apart," Daisy told them. "Here, let me show you."

Anna and Reed got busy, but Kaya just stood staring at her trowel like she couldn't believe she was holding it.

"Come on, Kaya!" Reed used his tiny shovel to gently guide Kaya toward Daisy's plot. "You can do homework *and* other things at the same time. My nanny always says I can't, but she's wrong."

"We can even make it into a game." Anna

thought for a minute. "Okay. I've got one. It's called Ice Cream Shop. If you can dig the hole in a single shovel scoop, you get one point. Two points for a double scoop and three for a triple scoop. You have to try to get the lowest points possible."

"Fine. But we have to work on our speech. Seriously." Kaya shoved her trowel in the dirt and pulled it out roughly, then her face burst into a smile. "Hey," she said. "Single scoop! One point for me."

Reed stuck his trowel in the ground and shoveled a giant clump of dirt.

Anna smiled and shook her head. "That's way too much. We'll call that an Oops Scoop. Do-over!"

Reed smushed the dirt back down with his fingers, even giving it a couple extra smushes.

Then he shoveled another giant clump of dirt.

Kaya giggled. "You're Oops Scooping on purpose."

Reed squished the soil between his fingers and nodded. "Uh-huh."

Anna and Kaya kept digging while Reed made another Oops Scoop. Every time Anna made a hole deep enough, Daisy took one of the broccoli seedlings out of a plastic pot and handed the ball of dirt and roots to Anna.

Anna cupped each plant gently in her palms. The roots looked like a tangled knot of white strings. Anna knew they'd have to spread out and grab on to the new soil or the plants would die. She lowered each plant carefully into a hole and patted new dirt all around it. Then she leaned down and whispered softly, "I know it's scary moving someplace new, broccobabies,

but you can do it. Spread your roots!"

"Who are you talking to?" Reed squinted one eye up at Anna like she was cuckoo.

"Did you just say you have an idea for our speech?" Kaya leaned forward eagerly.

"No!" Anna felt her cheeks burning like two hot peppers. "I didn't say anything. I'm just planting."

She quickly went back to digging another hole.

"So what are everyone's speech ideas?" Kaya asked as she made a double scoop.

"Students should be allowed to prank their teachers," Reed announced. "It's educational."

Kaya rubbed her forehead with the back of her hand. "How about if kids clear the dishes every day for a month, they should at least be allowed to get a goldfish."

"That's practically the same as your last idea." Reed pointed his shovel at Anna. "What are *your* topics?"

"Recycling?" Anna said.

Reed and Kaya looked at each other. Anna knew what they were thinking. B-O-R-I-N-G.

"Okay. How about bugs are cool, not creepy?"

Kaya's whole body shivered, like she felt bugs crawling on her skin as she imagined it. "Do you have any other ideas?" she asked.

Anna shook her head, and the kids finished planting. When they were done, the tiny broccoli plants looked like a little green audience ready to listen to a speech.

Anna did have a third idea. A new one. It had come to her while she was planting. But she wasn't sure she was ready to share it yet.

"At least that was fun," Anna said.

"Really fun!" Reed said.

"It wasn't that bad," Kaya admitted, "but what about our speech?"

Anna bit her lip. Sometimes when she had really big ideas, she got so excited she felt like they might just burst out of her, like air from a balloon. This was one of those ideas.

"You look like you have something to say," Kaya said, pointing at Anna. "Spill it!"

"Maybe we could do a speech about how much fun it is to work in a garden." Anna looked at Reed and Kaya. Neither of them said no, so she kept going. "We could start a kids' gardening club, and try to persuade our class to join."

"I like clubs," said Reed. "I'm already in a skateboard club and a magic club."

"We could build our own clubhouse and

grow watermelons and pumpkins." Anna paused. "And maybe even raise baby chicks?"

"Oooh, really? Baby chicks?" Kaya clasped her hands in front of her chest.

"Maybe." Anna shrugged. "We'd need to get our parents to let us do it."

The True-Blue Besties had dreamed about raising chicks before Anna moved, but no one's parents had actually approved it.

"I like it," said Reed, nodding his head.

"Baby chicks are so cute," said Kaya. Then she added, "Could I make a sign for our club?"

"Sure! So we all agree?" Anna asked.

Reed and Kaya nodded.

"Now we have to write our speech," Kaya said, then checked the pink plastic watch on her wrist. "But we don't have time today.

Hey, Daisy! Can we come to the garden again tomorrow?"

Daisy paused in her conversation with Maria and pretended to faint. "Of course. Tomorrow I'm harvesting cucumbers. I'll need lots of help."

Anna's heart did a little happy dance. Another day in the garden and the second day in a row of going home with a classmate. A smile spread across her face. Maybe her in-between-friends time had come to an end.

As Daisy walked Anna and Reed home, Kaya said, "I just thought of something. A club needs a name. What are we going to call it?"

This time Anna didn't worry about making a suggestion. She knew her name felt just right.

"We should call it the Friendship Garden."

CHAPTER 5

BLACK CLOUDS

All day Wednesday, Anna couldn't wait for school to end. For the past twenty-four hours she'd been thinking nonstop about the Friendship Garden. The night before, she'd talked about gardening all through dinner, then she'd dreamt that she was living inside a giant pumpkin, just like Peter Peter Pumpkin Eater's wife in the nursery rhyme.

Today she'd worn green pants with lots of pockets for tools, and sparkly rubber boots so she could really get into the dirt when she went to the garden after school.

At lunchtime, Outfit-Outfit Mackenzie said to Anna, "Hey, beetle girl, where are your tights today?" Her tone didn't sound friendly, and the other Outfit-Outfit girls were giggling, so Anna didn't show them the carrot socks hidden inside her boots.

When the bell rang, Anna, Kaya, and Reed raced to meet Daisy by the flagpole in front of school.

"I win!" Reed shouted, touching the flagpole with one hand.

"Lucky you!" said Daisy. "Your prize is pushing my cart. We'll use it to carry the vegetables we pick today."

"What?" Reed didn't look like he thought that was a very good prize, but he took the cart and began to walk up the sidewalk, weaving back and forth and making noises like a race car.

When they arrived at the garden, Daisy showed her helpers the cucumber vines. She taught them how to twist and pull the cucumbers off the plants. It wasn't as easy as it looked. If you didn't twist and pull just right, you might accidentally detach the whole vine from the fence.

When Daisy went to talk to Maria, Kaya said, "Hey, Anna, got any good cucumber-picking games?"

Anna rifled through the leaves to find her next cucumber. "Hmm. How about Counting Cucumbers? The first person will say 'I one the cucumber' as they pick, then the next person will pick and say, 'I two the cucumber.' Then the third person will say—"

"'I three the cucumber'!" Reed shouted, snapping a cucumber from the vine.

"Right," said Anna. "And whoever says 'I eight the cucumber' gets a point because they 'ate' the cucumber. Get it?"

"Got it," Kaya said, twisting and pulling with her whole body. Anna thought she made picking a cucumber look like a dance. "I one the cucumber!"

"You won?" Reed blew the hair off his forehead. "That was a fast game."

Kaya giggled. Then her face fell. "Wait a minute. I just thought of something. How can we have a garden club if we don't have a garden of our own?"

Reed picked two cucumbers and pretended like he was juggling. But he was really just tossing two cucumbers in the air and catching them. "Yeah," he said between catches. "We. Can't. Have. A. Club. With. No. Garden."

Anna frowned. She felt a black cloud form above her head. Kaya and Reed were right. What would the Friendship Garden do without an actual garden? Draw pictures of gardens? Watch movies about gardens?

N-O W-A-Y.

But where would they find a garden? Gardens didn't grow on trees. Anna stopped picking for a minute and pressed her fist against her mouth to think. There had to be someplace they could have a garden.

"Shoo! Go away!"

"Get out of here, you creeps!"

Anna was jolted out of her thoughts by two loud voices.

She looked up and saw Maria and a young girl with wavy brown hair running toward the plant junkyard shouting and flapping their hands. Two raccoons climbed out of the planting bed and raced down the alley behind the garden.

"Raccoons! Sweet!" Reed zoomed to the back fence and shouted again. "Hey, raccoons, come back!"

"They're so cute." Kaya ran to the fence too. "Why is everyone chasing them away?"

Anna followed Kaya and Reed.

"You think those pests are cute?" asked the wavy-haired girl. She looked a bit older than Anna, Kaya, and Reed. Anna remembered seeing her on the playground at school, but she hung out with the big kids. "I'm Simone, by the way, Maria's daughter, and raccoons are the absolute worst!"

"I'm Anna." Anna knew that while raccoons *could* be cute, in a garden they could also be big trouble. "Back in New York, my friends and I used to call raccoons Masked Munchers. If you don't pick your vegetables before they start to rot, raccoons sneak into your garden and help themselves."

"I'm Kaya, and I still think they're adorable," said Kaya.

"I just found out that the Duprees moved to Florida! Why didn't they tell me?" Maria said to Simone, throwing her hands in the air. "I've got to get this abandoned plot cleared out soon. Otherwise those raccoons are going to tell their friends. Before you know it, this place will turn into a raccoon den!" She pressed her finger to her chin. "Actually, maybe we'll tear out their plot altogether and build a shed there. We *do* need more storage around here."

Anna looked at all the sad old vegetables growing in the plot. What could have been beautiful tomatoes, peppers, cucumbers, and her favorite, sugar snap peas, were instead rotting and slimy. Yuck!

She walked closer, peering at the plot. *Some* of the crops were rotting, but not *all* of them. If only someone would clear out the weeds. If only someone would take care of it.

That was it! *"Psst!"* Anna whispered to Kaya and Reed.

She signaled for them to follow her to a

corner where no one would hear them. Maria went back into her shed, and Simone headed over to the water spigot and began to wind up a long black hose on a garden cart.

"What is it?" Reed asked. "Is it time to play a trick on Daisy? I've got some good ones. I always carry a rubber spider in my backpack for practical joke emergencies."

Kaya clucked her tongue. "There is no way you could fool Daisy with a rubber spider."

"This isn't a trick," said Anna, keeping her voice hushed. "It's an idea. What if we ask Maria to let us be in charge of the Duprees' old garden space? That would be the perfect spot for our club!"

Kaya wrinkled her nose as if she wasn't so sure. "But that plot is a mess. It will be too much work for us to clean it up."

"Did someone say too much work?" Reed shook his head. "I'm not a big fan of too much work."

"It won't be *that* much work. I'm actually a good gardener," Anna confessed. "I've gardened before."

"You have?" Kaya looked surprised.

"I guess we could try," Reed said slowly. "As long as I don't have to do too much work."

Anna held up one hand next to her shoulder like she was making a pledge. "Promise. Let's go tell Maria!"

They raced to the shed and knocked on the door.

"What's up, buttercups?" Maria asked, poking her head out.

"You don't have to tear down the Duprees' garden!" Anna's heart beat as fast as the chirps of Collin's windup toy crickets. She hadn't felt this excited about anything in a long time. "We found someone to take care of it for you."

"Really?" Maria stepped out of her shed, a great big smile on her face. "That's wonderful! Who?"

"Us!" Anna pointed at herself, then Kaya and Reed. "We are going to start a kids' gardening club and call it the Friendship Garden."

"We want to raise baby chicks," Kaya said.

"And play jokes with dirt that smells like diapers," Reed added.

Anna was about to explain that she knew all about gardening from helping her mom in New York. Then she noticed that Maria's smile didn't look like a smile anymore. It had turned into a thin line—like an inchworm. That *was* Anna's favorite creepy crawler, but only on flowers.

"I'm so sorry," Maria said, brushing some dirt off her pants, "but I can't let a group of kids run a plot in the garden."

Now Anna felt like a leaky balloon, shrinking S-L-O-W-L-Y.

"Actually, if you add all our ages together, we're really grown up," Reed said.

"And I'm very responsible." Kaya squared her shoulders and stood straight. "My mom said so."

"I'm sure you are," Maria said, "and I'd like to say yes." Her face really did look sad. "But garden rules say that every plot must be run by someone eighteen or older. Maybe you could find an adult to help you?"

Anna perked back up. She was sure she could find an adult to do just that.

"Let me know!" Maria said, and went back into her shed. Anna, Kaya, and Reed huddled together.

"Who should we ask?" Kaya whispered.

"Why are you whispering?" Reed whispered back.

"I don't know," Kaya whispered again. Then she laughed.

Anna poked her head out of the huddle and peeked over at Daisy pulling weeds. "I think Kaya should ask Daisy."

Reed and Anna followed Kaya over to her grandmother. Daisy was kneeling on a squishy purple square and she had a big pile of weeds next to her knees.

"Why, if it isn't my little helpers. I thought you'd deserted me."

Kaya looked back over her shoulder at Anna, then Reed. "Actually, Daisy, we were wondering if you could help us. We've decided to start our own gardening club."

"*Fabuloso!*" Daisy raised both hands, full of weeds, in the air. "I think that's a wonderful idea. And so do the sunflowers. Look, they're smiling!"

Reed leaned over and tapped Anna gently on the arm. Then he gave her a thumbs-up.

Kaya continued. "We want to take over the Duprees' old garden so that it doesn't get torn down. But Maria says kids aren't allowed to have their own plots. Could you be our official grown-up?"

Daisy lowered her arms, dropped the

weeds in the pile, and clapped the dirt from her hands. She turned to face them. "I'm sorry, *niños*, but I don't think I can handle two plots. Just one takes up most of my free time."

"We'll do all the work, Daisy!" Kaya clasped her hands together. "Promise!"

Daisy smacked her lips. "I'll tell you what. Why doesn't your club help me work on *my* garden? I can always use helpers. Today we'll start with weeding! Weeding is very exciting. You'll love it."

Daisy stood up, walked to the shed, and returned with three tools that looked like long forks with two prongs instead of three. She handed one to Anna, one to Reed, and one to Kaya.

"Poke the pointy end into the soil next to the stem, tilt it backward, and up pops the root." Daisy showed them with her own weeding tool. "*El trabajo es pan comido*. This work is a piece of cake. Easy-peasy, lemon squeezy!"

Anna, Kaya, and Reed started pulling weeds just the way Daisy showed them. Daisy nodded and said, "Excuse me, *niños*. I need to talk to Maria."

"This is supposed to be exciting? Daisy is crazy," Reed said.

"Yeah," Kaya agreed, scrunching her nose.

Anna actually liked pulling weeds. There was something very satisfying about pulling out each weed with its roots still attached, like little strings hanging down. Still, it would have been a lot more satisfying to pull her own weeds rather than Daisy's.

"Hey, guys!"

Anna looked up. There was Simone, hauling a wheelbarrow full of weeds and rotten vegetables to the compost bin in the alley. In the compost bin they would decompose and eventually turn into fertilizer for next year's garden.

"My mom told me about your idea," Simone said. "Are you really going to start a garden club?"

"Only if we can find a grown-up to help us." Reed pulled a weed and tossed it into Simone's wheelbarrow.

"Right now we're just garden helpers." Kaya sighed.

Simone tapped her foot against the wheelbarrow. "I've been trying to get my mom to let me have my own garden plot for years, but she said she's too busy to help me. I'll be in your club." She paused. "Even if I am two years older than you," she added.

Reed and Kaya frowned at that last part. But Anna's heart jumped when she thought of how close they were to having their own garden.

"Four of us could definitely handle that plot all by ourselves!" she exclaimed. "I wish the grown-ups could see that it wouldn't be *work* to help us."

"You'll just have to persuade them." Simone lifted the handles of her wheelbarrow and headed to the alley. Then she let out a little scream.

Reed gave Anna and Kaya a playful grin. He jumped up and grabbed a big black rubber spider from the wheelbarrow. He waved it at Simone. "Don't freak out! It's fake!"

Simone folded her arms across her chest. "I wouldn't scream about a dumb fake spider. Look!" She pointed across the lot at the Duprees' old plant junkyard, where Maria stood talking to a man with a big belly. He wore muddy work boots and was stretching a tape measure across the garden bed.

Simone whipped her head around and stared at Anna with wide eyes. "That's Oscar! He helps build things in the garden sometimes. My mom said she was going to ask him to tear down the Duprees' old plot. You better persuade her fast or our garden's a goner!"

"Let's each ask our parents tonight," said Kaya, turning to Anna and Reed.

Great, thought Anna. Now she had to write *two* persuasive speeches.

CHAPTER 6

COUNTING GREEN BEANS

That evening after she had put on pajamas, Anna planned a persuasive speech while she watered her plants. Only, this one wasn't for school.

"I've gardened before," Anna told Fern. "I can be in charge of everything."

"Our grown-up helper wouldn't *actually* need to help," she said to Chloe.

"He or she could just sit in a chair and read," she added, rotating Spike's pot to face the window. "After all, I take good care of the three of you."

When her small red watering can was empty, Anna set it on the windowsill next to Fern, Chloe, and Spike. She wondered what Kaya and Reed would say if they knew she talked to plants. She wondered what the Outfit-Outfit would say. Then she decided that she didn't want to know.

Anna climbed into bed, pulled her comforter up, and waited. She could hear her parents in Collin's room singing his good-night song, the same one they'd sung every night since he was a baby.

A minute later she heard footsteps in the hallway, then Anna's father opened her bedroom door. He carried his cell phone out in front of him. Anna could see her mother's face on the screen.

"Hi, Anna Banana," her mom said. "Did you have a good day?"

"Really good!" Anna shifted onto her knees so she had a better view of her mom. "My gardening club found the perfect spot for a garden of our own."

"That's great!" Anna's father ruffled Anna's hair with his free hand.

"Where is it?" Anna's mother leaned a little closer to the camera.

"In the plant junkyard in the Shoots and Leaves Community Garden. It used to belong to a family named the Duprees, but they moved away. If we get rid of all the weeds and rotting vegetables, we can make

it grow again. It just needs to be cleaned up."

Suddenly Anna wished her mother hadn't leaned so close to the camera, because it made her frown look extra huge. "That sounds like an awful lot of work, Banana."

"Our club already has four members," Anna said. "It won't be that much work if we do it together. The True-Blue Besties had a garden."

"It's great that you want to do this," began her father, "but your mother's right. This is much bigger than the little square you, Hayley, and Lauren had in New York. I'm surprised Shoots and Leaves is willing to go along with it."

Anna tugged the sleeves of her pajamas. "Well, Maria, that's the garden president, she thinks it's a great idea, as long as—" Anna stopped and made direct eye contact with her parents. Direct eye contact was when you looked right at your audience. Mr. Hoffman claimed it was very important in persuasive speeches. "As long as we find a grown-up to help us."

Mr. Fincher smiled. "That shouldn't be too hard. What about Kaya's grandmother? What's her name? Daisy?"

Anna tapped her chin. "Daisy says it would be too much work for her. She's already got a garden to take care of."

"I'm sorry, sweetie," said Anna's mother. "I'm sure you'll find someone."

Anna smiled. (Mr. Hoffman said smiling was a big part of persuading people too.) "I *know* I'll find someone," said Anna. "And it's you! You know all about gardening and growing food." Anna turned to her father. "And you used to help mom in the garden every weekend. Remember your rake dance?" Anna had always loved it when her father had pretended to dance with the rakes.

Anna's mom shook her head. "I'm sorry, honey. I would help if I could, but I've got my hands full at the new restaurant. I just don't have the time."

"It wouldn't take much time," Anna insisted. "Reed, Kaya, and I would do all the work!"

"But you can't be in the garden unsupervised." Her mother tilted her head and put her fingers up to the camera of her phone. "I wish I could give you a hug."

"*You* could supervise us," Anna told her father. "You're at home most of the day."

Anna's father gave her a hug. "I'm sorry too, but that would be a big job. And I can't take that kind of extra responsibility right now. I'm still getting used to my *new* job: running things here at home and cooking dinners. Plus, I have to watch Collin as well as you. Maybe we can try it in the spring when I'm more used to things."

The spring? That might as well be a million years away! The plant junkyard wouldn't even be there in the spring! Oscar would tear it down and put a big ugly shed in its place. The Friendship Garden would be finished before it even began.

"Please?" Anna hugged herself tightly and looked back and forth between her parents.

"I'm so sorry, Banana." Her mom really

did look sad. "I know moving hasn't been easy for you. I wish I could help, but I can't."

"I'm not saying no," said Dad, "I'm saying *not right now*."

Anna swallowed the lump in her throat. Didn't they understand? *Right now* was the only time she had.

"Are you ready for your good-night song?" Anna's mother asked. "It's almost time for me to get back to work."

Anna nodded. Once again she had failed to persuade her parents.

Her father tucked her in and then her mother began to sing the song they had sung to her every single night since she was a baby. After the first few lines, her father joined in too. The song was called "The Garden Song," and Anna's parents had even written a special verse just for her.

Inch by inch,
Row by row,
Anna helps our garden grow.
With her little rake and hoe,
She plants seeds in the ground.
Inch by inch,
Row by row,
Anna helps our garden grow.
Waters, waits, and sings real low
To her plants below the ground.

Ever since Anna was little she loved going to sleep imagining the inches and inches and rows and rows of growing flowers and vegetables. Other kids might count sheep, but Anna counted string beans.

Tonight, for the first time since she had

found out they were moving, the bedtime song made her feel sad. After her parents kissed her good night and her father turned out the light, Anna rolled over on her side. She stared out the window at the moon. How long would it be before she got to work in her very own garden again? At this rate, she might have to wait until she was a grown-up!

Anna closed her eyes. One green bean. Two green beans. By ten she fell asleep.

CHAPTER 7

SILVER LININGS

The next day at school Mr. Hoffman reminded his students that tomorrow each group would present their speeches to the class.

"Don't forget, a good persuasive speech has solid evidence, or proof from experts, but it also has emotion. You want your audience to *feel* convinced."

The bell rang for recess. Anna, Kaya, and Reed gave one another panicked looks.

"Let's meet by the swings," Kaya suggested. "We need to talk about our speech."

Anna knew Kaya must mean business. Usually Kaya drew under the cottonwood tree during recess.

"Any luck with your parents?" Kaya asked as she kicked her swing off the ground. "My parents said they are too busy at their FroYo shop."

Reed moved to lie on the swing with his head propped up on his hands. "I asked my parents if they would help, but my mom said if I want fresh vegetables, she'll order them from a farm that will deliver to our house every week. Ew. I don't want to eat them, I just want to grow them!"

"Will *your* parents help?" Kaya asked.

Anna shook her head.

"This is terrible." Kaya pumped her swing higher and higher, then looked down at Anna and Reed. "We're supposed to give our speech tomorrow. We can't persuade everyone to join our garden club when we don't have a garden to garden in!"

Anna knew that Kaya was right. "We have to get that garden," she said.

She lifted her feet from the ground and spun around in a circle as her swing untwisted itself.

"Hey, garden buddies!"

Anna looked up. Simone stood by the playground fence with a group of fifth-grade girls. She waved at Anna, Kaya, and Reed.

"Those are the little kids I was telling you

about," Simone told her friends. "They're going to help me get a garden."

"The garden is for *all* of us," Anna whispered to Kaya and Reed.

"And we're not little," Reed added.

"We're littler than she is," Kaya said. Anna and Reed couldn't argue with that.

"Hold on a second," Simone called to her friends. She jogged over to the swings.

"Did you find us a grown-up?"

"Nope," said Anna.

"It's hopeless," said Kaya.

"All the grown-ups think it's too much work," Reed said. "I guess they don't like work either."

Simone frowned. "We need to prove they're wrong."

Anna stopped swinging. She put her feet on the ground. "We *can* prove it. We just have to clean up the Duprees' plot all by ourselves. If the garden isn't rotting anymore, would your mom still tear it down?"

"I don't think so," Simone said, starting to smile.

"But how can we clean it?" Reed pulled himself up and stood on the seat of his swing. "The grownups already said no."

"Maybe we could do it in secret," Anna said. "No one would be mad if we did a good job."

"In secret?" Kaya dragged her feet on the ground until she stopped swinging. "I don't think you can clean up a garden without people seeing you."

"You can if no one is there." Simone tapped her chin with a blue fingernail. "My mom always goes to her Zumba class on Saturday mornings, and I have a garden key. I'll meet you there at ten o'clock."

"But how will we work there? My parents won't let me stay alone," Reed said.

"Me neither," Anna said.

"Daisy works in the garden on Saturday mornings," Kaya said. "She could watch us, but we won't be able to keep it a secret from her."

"We won't have to," Simone said. "We'll just tell her my mom said it was okay."

Anna wasn't sure she liked the sound of that. It seemed like a lie, and lies were wrong.

Then again, this was important. If they did a good job, everyone would understand, and she *knew* they could do a good job.

"Okay," said Anna. "Let's do it!"

"Great." Simone nodded toward her fifth-grade group. "I have to get back to my friends. Don't forget, we'll have one hour to clean everything up. See you on Saturday."

"One hour?" That was impossible. Anna knew they couldn't clean up the entire garden plot in one hour. Not with only four people.

She turned to Kaya and Reed. "We are going to need a lot more help."

"I think we need to change the topic of our speech," Kaya decided.

"What do you mean?" Reed asked. "We almost have our own garden. Why would we change our topic now?"

"Because we need to persuade the class to come to the garden on Saturday morning to help us!"

That afternoon Kaya and Reed came over to Anna's house to finish their speech. Her father baked zucchini spice muffins for a snack—Anna's favorite! Her mother had created that recipe in Rosendale when their garden produced too much zucchini.

"You're going to love these!" Anna told

Kaya and Reed. "Even if you don't like vegetables," she added when she saw Reed's face. "They don't *taste* like zucchini."

Reed picked the biggest muffin on the platter and peeled back the paper liner. He shrugged. "I love every muffin I eat," he said, taking a giant bite. He chewed a couple of times, then the side of his nose twitched up.

"What?" Anna took a bite. This did not taste like her mom's muffins. Instead of being moist and sweet, it was dry and bitter. "Dad?" she asked with a frown. "Did you use Mom's recipe?"

"Of course!" He held up the yellow binder where Anna's mom kept all her best recipes. "I followed it exactly. Well, sort of. I made a few of my own adjustments."

Mr. Fincher picked up a muffin and took a

big bite. He chewed for a while. "They might need some more adjustments," he remarked with his mouth full.

Anna's father took away the muffins and put out a bowl of pretzels instead. When Anna and her friends finished eating, they got to work on their speech. Anna was in charge of listing the reasons why gardening is important for kids.

"Let's tell everyone that if they help, they can pick their very own vegetable to take home!" Anna suggested.

"We want people to help," Reed said, shaking his head, "not run away screaming. Who wants a free vegetable?"

Kaya patted Anna on the shoulder. "I think it's a good idea, but maybe we could also give out coupons for a free frozen yogurt at FroYo Go. My parents are always trying to get me to pass those out."

Reed held out his hand. "I'll take twenty, please."

Anna giggled. "All right. Back to work."

Reed made a list of all the ways gardening was fun instead of hard work. Kaya made a list of how gardening helped kids learn. Then she drew a beautiful poster that said *The Friendship Garden*. The poster had ivy around the edges and a vegetable garden in the middle. Yellow baby chicks and striped raccoons played in the leaves. Anna and Reed helped color it in.

When Anna got ready for bed that night, she whispered quietly to her plants as she watered them. "I think this might work. I might actually have a garden." She smiled. "And new friends."

Ever since she'd moved to Chicago, Anna had felt like her skies had been filled with gray clouds. If she could make the Friendship Garden work, though, those clouds might have a shiny silver lining.

CHAPTER 8

SIX GREEN THUMBS-UP

The next day at school Mr. Hoffman pushed the desks around the edges of the classroom so that everyone would have room to give their persuasive speech. Anna politely listened to Jessica, Carlos, and Nina talk about the importance of flossing your teeth, and Sarah, Jamie, and Michael discuss bringing lunch in reusable containers instead of plastic bags. Her knee bounced up and down as she listened. *Bounce, bounce, bounce.* Her mom called it Anna's Bouncy Knee, but it only came out when she was nervous about something. Anna hoped her classmates would like her speech, and she hoped they would all be persuaded to help clean up the garden. Bouncy Knee apparently hoped so too.

When Mr. Hoffman finally called her name, Anna's heart fluttered like a leaf in a breeze. She stood up and looked at Kaya and Reed. They both gave her two green thumbs-up. Anna smiled when she saw the green face paint they had used to color the skin on their thumbs. She gave them two green thumbs-up too. All three of them stepped to the front of the classroom.

"Do you have a green thumb?" Anna asked

her classmates. She, Kaya, and Reed gave the class six green thumbs-up. Mr. Hoffman had told them to start with an attention grabber. "If you don't, we'll tell you how to get one."

"Kids who garden boost their brain power." Kaya tapped her finger on the side of her head. "They understand nature better when they plant seeds and watch them grow. But being in a garden teaches you about more than just plants. You also get to learn about animals, weather, soil, and building things."

"Plus," Reed added as he stepped forward, "gardening isn't just work. It's also fun. You get to be outside. You get to dig. And you do it with your friends."

Reed pointed to Anna and Kaya when he said that last part, and Anna's whole body felt warm, as if she were standing in a patch of summer sunlight.

"Having a garden is a *little* like having a pet." Anna felt the words spilling out of her mouth with extra excitement. She might have two new friends! She almost had a garden! "It can be a lot of responsibility to take care of something that is alive. But it's also really cool when you see your garden sprout and bloom." The more Anna spoke, the more excited she felt. This was going to work. They were going to convince everyone that gardening is great. They'd surely have help tomorrow when they cleaned up the Duprees' plant junkyard, and then Maria would let them have their club. Anna would have more friends than pumpkins in a pumpkin patch!

"Actually," Anna continued, her mouth going so fast she could hardly control what was coming out, "having a garden is a *lot* like having a pet. You can even talk to your plants when you take care of them. I talk to my plants all the time. It helps them grow."

As soon as the words left Anna's mouth, she wished she could eat them back up again. The entire class began to laugh.

"Talk to plants?" Mackenzie looked at the Outfit-Outfit. She twirled her finger around her ear in the cuckoo sign.

"What do you say to them?" shouted a boy named Will. "'Hi, tree, can I pick one of your apples?'"

Suddenly Anna wished she could hide behind Mr. Hoffman's desk.

"Okay, class," said Mr. Hoffman. "Everyone settle down, please."

When the class got quiet, Mr. Hoffman asked Anna, Kaya, and Reed if they had anything else to add.

"Only that if you'd like to give gardening a try, you should come to the Shoots and Leaves Community Garden tomorrow at ten o'clock." Kaya held up the flyer that she and Anna had made on Anna's computer. "We're starting a kids' gardening club called the Friendship Garden and you are all invited to help. Oh, and everyone who comes get a free frozen yogurt from my parents' store, FroYo Go. With unlimited toppings," she added.

Excited murmurs rippled through the room.

"But remember," Reed added, "it will be the fun kind of helping. Not hard-work helping."

Reed and Kaya looked at Anna, but she didn't want to add anything else. She was afraid to even open her mouth. What if more weird sentences starting coming out? Anna doubted if anyone could be convinced to help now that they thought she was strange.

"Great speech, folks," said Mr. Hoffman. "Why don't you put your flyers in everyone's mailboxes?"

Anna helped Reed and Kaya pass out the flyers.

"Why did you add that part about talking to plants?" Kaya whispered. "That wasn't part of the speech."

"Do you really talk to plants?" Reed asked.

"It does help them grow," Anna explained with a shrug. She didn't add that it probably wouldn't help them find new club members.

Just before ten the next morning, Anna's parents and Collin walked Anna over to Shoots and Leaves. Kaya and Simone were waiting for Anna at the gate. Mr. and Mrs. Fincher waved to Daisy, then they took Collin to the playground two blocks away.

"My mom just left," Simone whispered. "Are you guys ready?"

Anna peered over Simone's shoulder. "Is Reed here yet? Has anyone else come to help?"

Kaya shook her head. "I'm sure Reed will

show up any minute. Until he gets here, we'll just have to work double-time."

Anna, Kaya, and Simone closed the garden gate and walked toward the back.

"You girls want to help me pick my radishes?" Daisy called.

"They're going to help me today," Simone called back. "My mom said we could start clearing the Duprees' old plot."

"She did?" Daisy stood up and scratched her chin. "Maria didn't mention that to me."

Next to her, Anna heard Kaya gulp. Anna knew Kaya felt terrible that they weren't telling Daisy the truth. But it was the only way they'd get a chance to prove they could handle the garden.

Simone scratched her head. "Um, it was a last-minute decision."

She then grabbed three weeding tools and two canvas buckets from the shed. "Let's dig in!" she said.

The three girls got to work, poking the weeding tools into the soil, tilting them back, and popping out weed after weed. Every time they removed a weed, they tossed it into one of the canvas buckets sitting on the path between them. Anna smiled as she pulled up each weed with its thick tangle of roots. It was the most satisfying feeling in the world!

Every now and then Kaya would ask either Anna or Simone if a certain plant was a weed or not. Once she almost removed a zucchini plant and twice she nearly took out the Brussels sprouts. When both baskets were full, Anna and Simone emptied them in the compost bin in the alley.

"What time is it?" Anna asked.

Simone checked her phone. "Ten thirty."

Anna shook her head. "We've barely cleared one quarter of the garden, but half our time is already up. We'll never finish before Maria gets back!"

Simone bit her lip. She looked as worried as Anna felt, but she said, "We can do it. Maybe Reed's here by now."

Anna hoped so. She couldn't believe Reed hadn't come. She guessed he'd decided it was too much hard work after all. Or maybe he didn't actually want to be friends with someone who talked to plants.

Simone tucked her bucket against her hip and went back to the garden, but Anna stayed in the alley for an extra minute. She felt prickles at the back of her eyelids and wanted to be alone in case she started crying. Anna blinked a bunch of times to clear the tears away. She took a long, shaky breath.

Then she heard a scream.

CHAPTER 9

BEADY BLACK EYES

Anna rushed back to the garden. Her heart was pattering even faster than her footsteps.

"Shoo!" Simone was shouting. "Get OUT!"

Anna's eyes darted left and right, trying to figure out what was going on.

Just then, four raccoons tumbled over the side of the Duprees' garden bed. Instead of escaping back into the alley like last time, they ran straight for Daisy's garden.

"Daisy! Look out," Kaya shouted.

Daisy jumped up and grabbed a rake. She waved it in the direction of the raccoons, who turned, ran into a big plot in the center of the garden, and hid under some bushy water-melon vines.

Kaya rushed over to Anna, who stood fro-zen at the back of the garden. "When I started weeding by the string beans," Kaya said with a gasp, "I pulled up a giant weed and saw a pair of beady black eyes staring at me. My hair almost stood straight up! It's the first time I didn't think a raccoon was cute. They must have been living in the Duprees' garden!"

Simone grabbed a hose, pulled it over to

the plot where the raccoons were hiding, and started spraying the watermelon vines. The critters leaped from their hiding place, trailing muddy paw prints everywhere they went. Simone followed them with the hose, but the raccoons raced from garden plot to garden plot, knocking over the wheelbarrow, spraying clumps of mud, and making a big old M-E-S-S everywhere they went.

"What's going on?" A voice shouted from the front of the garden.

Anna's heart skipped a beat. Simone froze. Kaya squeaked. They all looked at the front gate.

It was Reed! And with him stood a woman Anna guessed was his nanny, six other students from their class, and Mr. Hoffman.

"We thought you weren't coming!" Anna cried.

Simone turned off the hose.

"I decided to make a few stops on my way." Reed pointed to the kids standing behind him. "I thought it might persuade them more if I passed out the coupons early."

"Did you go to Mr. Hoffman's house?" Kaya's eyes were as round as tomatoes. She put her hand over her mouth. She looked like she couldn't believe anyone would do something as crazy as going to a *teacher's* house.

Reed wrinkled his eyebrows and shook his head. "No way. We just found him on the sidewalk in front of the garden."

"I thought I'd stop by and see how the Friendship Garden cleanup project was going,"

Mr. Hoffman said. He looked around at the mishmash of dirt, plants, and children, then rocked back and forth on his heels. "Aren't any grown-ups helping you?"

"My *abuela*'s here." Kaya pointed at her grandmother, who was marching around the edge of the garden searching for the raccoons. She waved her rake at Mr. Hoffman.

"We don't need grown-ups," Anna said. "I mean, we need a little grown-up help today, but not because we can't do it. Just because we don't have a lot of time."

"Well, I'll help." Mr. Hoffman pushed up the sleeves of his sweatshirt. Anna had never seen him without a bow tie. It was definitely weird to see a teacher outside of school

wearing what Anna's mother called "weekend clothes." "Am I allowed to help even if I am a grown-up?" he asked.

"Of course," said Anna. She looked at Reed and the other students standing behind them. "Thank you all for coming," she added, remembering to be polite. Then she turned to Simone. "How much time do we have left?"

Simone furrowed her eyebrows. "Only fifteen minutes."

Anna took a deep breath and put her hands on her hips. "Okay everyone, first things first. The Masked Munchers are hiding in that garden bed," she pointed to a tangle of vines. "We have to get them out. I have a plan."

Anna told everyone to hold hands and form a line so their bodies stretched from the left side of the garden to the right. They didn't quite reach all the way, so Anna asked Daisy to help too.

"Okay," said Daisy, "but don't get too close. Raccoons will attack if they feel threatened."

Anna took a deep breath. She knew what to do. "I'm going to shoo the raccoons, but when they run out, don't chase them! Stay in line, stomp your feet, shout, and march toward the alley. I think the raccoons will run away from us, so we have to make sure that the only way they can go is out of the garden. Everyone got it?"

Anna heard a bunch of yeahs and yesses and one *si*.

She grabbed a rake, stepped over to the plot where she had last seen the raccoons, and started rustling the plants. As soon as the raccoons popped out of the leaves, everyone started stomping and shooing and marching, just like Anna had told them to.

The raccoons raced for the back of the garden, squeezed under the fence, and took off down the alley.

"Hooray!" Anna jumped up and down. Simone and Kaya hugged.

"We did it!" said Reed, high-fiving Carlos, one of the boys he brought to help.

"Now what?" said Mr. Hoffman.

Anna pushed her sleeves up to her elbows, just like Mr. Hoffman had done earlier. "Now we weed."

Simone and Kaya found more weeding tools in the shed, and Anna and Reed taught Mr. Hoffman, Carlos, and the other students how to use them. Soon everyone was working and laughing, and the weed buckets filled up faster than Anna could empty them.

While they worked, Anna taught everyone the words to "The Garden Song"—though she left out the verse her parents had made up. Reed pranked Mr. Hoffman by placing a rubber snake in the dirt.

"Yipes!" yelled Mr. Hoffman, hopping out of the plot with his hands in the air. "A snake!"

Anna giggled as Reed showed Mr. Hoffman that the snake was a fake.

"Oh, heh-heh," Mr. Hoffman said shakily. "Um, I'm not a fan of snakes." He wiped his forehead with the sleeve of his sweatshirt.

"Well, Anna Banana, it looks like you're running quite an operation!"

Anna looked up from the bucket she was hauling to the compost bin and saw her parents walking into the garden with Collin.

She froze. *Her parents?!* That must mean it was almost eleven o'clock.

Anna's chest tightened. She scanned the Duprees' old plot. It looked much better than it used to, but it still wasn't completely cleaned up. And they were running out of—

"What's this?" Suddenly Maria appeared, walking in behind Anna's parents. She stood with her hands on her hips and a big frown on her face. She was wearing a leopard-print shirt and shiny black leggings. "Who's having a party in my garden that I wasn't invited to?"

Oops. They were already out of time.

Out of the corner of her eye, Anna saw

that Reed, Kaya, and Simone had turned into statues.

Maria's eyes inspected every inch of the garden. Finally they landed on Simone.

"Simone, do you mind telling me what's going on here?" she asked.

Simone laid her weeding tool on the ground, then took a step forward. "I wanted to prove to you that kids can handle a garden. You would never let me have my own plot, and you wouldn't let the Friendship Garden have one either. But we *can* take care of it. Look!"

Simone pointed to the Duprees' old plot. One end of it still resembled a wild jungle, but the rest held tidy rows of vegetables and greens. Each row even had a Popsicle stick tucked into the dirt with a tiny picture of the vegetable that was growing there: tomatoes, zucchini, and pumpkins. Kaya had made them.

"You didn't have permission to do that." Maria shook her head. "The Duprees' old plot looks great, but what about the rest of Shoots and Leaves? It looks like a tornado went through it."

Daisy put her hand on Kaya's shoulder and turned her around. "You told me you had Maria's permission."

Kaya's chin began to quiver. "I'm sorry."

Anna looked at her parents. They were both frowning and her mother had her arms folded across her chest. "Anna, we're disappointed," she said.

Anna's knees began to shake. "It's all my fault," she confessed. "I knew it was wrong to lie, but I wanted the Friendship Garden so badly. I thought it would be okay if I proved what good gardeners we were. I'm sorry, too."

She grabbed the overturned wheelbarrow and put it right side up.

Maria stroked Simone's hair and smiled at Anna. "I know you all can take care of a garden," she said. "You are wonderful helpers here. But Shoots and Leaves has rules and I have to follow them. As much as I would love to let you all take care of this garden, I can't. Not unless you have an adult who is willing to take full responsibility."

Anna felt a lump in her throat that wouldn't budge, no matter how hard she swallowed. She knew that Maria had to follow the rules. And deep down inside she knew that this wasn't a silly rule. Still, she couldn't help feeling that it just wasn't fair!

She had to give up her home, her best friends, and her garden back in Rosendale. And now she had to give up her garden in Chicago and her chance at new friends.

"You know," said Daisy. "It was the rotten raccoons who made the mess, not the *niños*. *El que tiene boca se equivoca*. We all make mistakes."

Daisy gave Kaya a hug.

"Ehem." Mr. Hoffman cleared his throat and held out a hand for Maria to shake. "I'm Grant Hoffman. I teach at Sullivan Magnet School. Yesterday these kids persuaded me that gardening can be an important tool for learning." Mr. Hoffman faced Anna, Kaya, Reed, and the other volunteers. "I'd love to be the adult chaperone for the Friendship

Garden, but I have two conditions. First, we'd have to make it an official school club. That means anyone from Sullivan would be able to join. Is that okay with you, kids?"

Anna locked gazes with Kaya and Reed. They didn't have to say a word. She could read the yesses in their smiles and twinkling eyes, just the way she used to be able to with Lauren and Hayley.

"The more the merrier," Anna said.

"Great." Mr. Hoffman raised his eyes to the adults. "And second, would you all be willing to take turns helping out in the afternoons? Maybe once or twice a week?"

"I'm here most days already," Daisy said. "I could help once a week."

"I could too," Maria added.

"What do you say, Collin?" Mr. Fincher asked Anna's brother. "Would you like to garden one day a week?"

Collin nodded his head, then tugged his father's shirt and asked, "Will there be worms? The biggest worm ever found was longer than two cars."

Mr. Fincher made a face. "There will be worms, but hopefully the short kind."

"Well then, kids." Maria smiled at Anna, Kaya, Reed, and Simone. "It looks like you've got yourselves a garden."

Anna pumped her fist in the air. "Yes!" She turned to the Duprees' old plot. The plant junkyard. No, it wasn't either of those things anymore. It was the Friendship Garden.

She looked at the plants and smiled. "Did you hear that? You're safe!"

"Uh, Anna," Simone asked. "Who are you talking to?"

Anna was so happy she didn't even feel embarrassed. "To the plants!" she said.

"It helps them grow," Kaya explained.

Reed bent over and whispered to a small green pumpkin. "I'm going to help you be the biggest pumpkin in the whole universe!" He looked at Anna. "Do they like music?"

Anna nodded. "I make up special songs for mine at home sometimes."

Reed grinned. "I'm going to write a pumpkin rap."

Simone laughed and stroked the string beans. "Hi, Beanie, nice to meet you."

"So, Anna, you've got your garden and a bunch of friends to garden with." Her dad gestured at all the kids standing around Shoots and Leaves. "Now what?"

Anna smiled and pointed to the section of the Friendship Garden that still looked like a jungle. "Now we finish weeding!"

That night Anna helped her father cook zucchini fritters with freshly picked zucchini from the Friendship Garden. She made him follow Mom's recipe exactly. Well, almost exactly—Anna made an adjustment or two of her own.

"Mmmm," said Collin, taking a big bite, "these are good. Maybe even better than Mom's."

"Really?" said Anna's father. His mouth dropped in surprise as he set the chicken on the table, sat down in his seat, and took a bite himself. "They *are* good," he agreed. "Well, what do you know? I guess my cooking is getting better. Maybe I just needed fresher ingredients. Looks like I'm lucky to have such a good gardener for a daughter."

Anna smiled and took a bite of her own fritter. Mmm. She closed her eyes. Now *that* tasted like home.

ACTIVITY: **GROW YOUR OWN BROCCOBABIES!**

Want to grow broccobabies just like Daisy? Follow the directions below!

What you will need:

Six empty yogurt cups

Potting soil

Broccoli seeds

A sunny window

Water

What you will do:

Planting all depends on weather, so you will need to look up your city in an almanac. The almanac will tell you what day in spring the last expected frost will be. Plan to start your seedlings six weeks before that day.

To start your broccobabies, poke a few holes in the bottom of each yogurt cup for drainage, then fill each cup with potting soil.

Next, press a dimple in the top of the soil with your finger and add a few broccoli seeds, then fill the dimple with soil.

Sprinkle your seeds with water.

When the seeds start to sprout, remove the smallest ones so that each cup only has one seedling.

Place your cups in a sunny window, and water or mist every day to keep the soil moist but not wet. Don't overwater.

Two weeks before the day of your last frost, you can go ahead and plant your broccobabies in the ground. Just remove the seedlings from the yogurt cups and dig a hole for each of them about six inches apart in your garden, or transplant them to bigger containers outside if you don't have a garden.

Oh!

One more thing.

Don't forget to sing and talk to your plants.

RECIPE: **ANNA'S ZUCCHINI FRITTERS**

Now you can make zucchini fritters that are just as tasty as Anna's. Be sure to ask your parents to help you in the kitchen!

Ingredients:

2 medium zucchini, grated

$\frac{1}{2}$ teaspoon kosher salt, plus more for seasoning

1 small onion, grated

1 large egg

$\frac{1}{4}$ cup all-purpose flour

1 tablespoon cornstarch

Freshly ground black pepper

Olive oil cooking spray

Baking instructions:

Preheat oven to 400 degrees.

Place the grated zucchini in a colander. Toss it with ½ teaspoon salt. Set the colander in the sink and let it stand ten minutes. Then press the zucchini with a paper towel to release as much liquid as possible.

Place the dry zucchini in a large bowl and gently mix in onion, egg, flour, and cornstarch. Season with salt and pepper.

Spray a cookie sheet with olive oil, then drop spoonfuls of the zucchini mixture a couple inches apart. Bake for ten minutes, then flip the fritters and bake for ten minutes more.

Serve with a spoonful of sour cream or applesauce for dipping.

ACKNOWLEDGMENTS

This garden wouldn't have bloomed without the help of so many.

Jennifer Mattson for planting the seed.

Amy Cloud and all the fine gardeners at Aladdin for pulling the weeds.

Brenda Ferber, Carolyn Crimi, Laura Ruby, Mary Loftus, and Sarah Aronson for pruning.

Lynn Hydman and Dawes Elementary School, and Jeanne Nolan and everyone at the Organic Gardener for much-needed fertilization.

And finally, Peter, Emma, Adam, and Noah for being my air and rain and sunshine.

Find out what happens in

THE FRIENDSHIP GARDEN

Book 2: *Pumpkin Spice*.

CHAPTER 1

PERFECT PUMPKIN

Reed wrapped both of his arms around the biggest pumpkin in the Friendship Garden.

"Um, Reed," said Anna, as she picked a withered zucchini plant, "I know that some gardeners talk and sing to plants to help them grow, but I've never heard of anyone hugging a plant."

Reed stretched the tips of his fingers just a bit farther until they touched. Then he let go of the pumpkin. "I wasn't hugging it. I was *measuring* it."

"Does measuring a pumpkin help it grow?" asked Kaya as she removed the Popsicle sticks that had labeled all of the garden's plants. It was almost the end of October. Nothing much was growing anymore.

"Don't you guys remember?" Reed pointed to the flyer hanging on the Shoots and Leaves Community Garden bulletin board. "The Windy City Pumpkin Fest is this Sunday, and I want to win the prize for biggest pumpkin."

"*You* want to win?" Kaya asked him accusingly. "You mean *we* want to win!"

Reed's cheeks turned pink. "I mean I want the Friendship Garden to win. Herbert just needs to grow a little bit bigger."

"Herbert?" Kaya scratched her head. "Who names a pumpkin Herbert?"

Anna studied Herbert. He was the biggest and roundest pumpkin in the Friendship Garden's pumpkin patch. As far as Anna was concerned, Herbert was pretty much P-E-R-F-E-C-T.

When Anna had first moved to Chicago from upstate New York, she didn't think she'd ever get to have her own garden again. But then Anna met Kaya and Reed, and the three of them started a gardening club called the Friendship Garden. Mr. Hoffman, their third-grade teacher, was the grown-up in charge, and they grew all their vegetables at Shoots and Leaves, the community garden in their neighborhood.

In Chicago, many people didn't have room for gardens in their backyards. In fact, a lot of people didn't even have backyards, so sometimes empty lots were turned into growing spaces. There, different neighbors had their own plots of land to plant flowers and vegetables.

"What about Mr. Eggers's pumpkins? That one in the corner of his plot looks pretty big." Anna tilted her head toward the front of Shoots and Leaves. Mr. Eggers was an old man with silver curly hair and a bushy mustache. He was trimming back pumpkin vines, but just then he looked up and frowned at the kids in the Friendship Garden.

"His pumpkin isn't round like Herbert. It's much narrower, but a lot taller," Kaya whispered, "and it might be bigger too. It's hard to tell."

"Okay, everyone, time for a break!" Mr. Hoffman set up his three-legged gardening stool and beckoned for the kids to gather around.

Anna followed Kaya and Reed over to Mr. Hoffman. Next to him stood Simone, a fifth grader whose mom, Maria, was the president of Shoots and Leaves. That meant Maria was in charge of the whole garden.

"Great work today." Mr. Hoffman pulled a brown clipboard from his backpack. "I think we are right on target for putting the garden to bed for the winter. Why don't all the teams give me a report? Bailey? How about your group?"

"We were in charge of clearing out the

broccoli," Bailey said proudly, pointing to a small section at the front of the Friendship Garden. "They were really easy to pull up."

"But there was so much dirt!" said Mackenzie, wrinkling her nose. "Right, Bay?"

Bailey looked back and forth between Mr. Hoffman and Mackenzie. Finally she wrinkled her nose too. "Yeah, tons of dirt."

"It kept spilling on our shoes," said Mackenzie, pointing at the matching pairs of silver-and-white sneakers on her and Bailey's feet. "We *just* got these."

Kaya leaned over to Anna and muttered, her eyes sparkling. "What a surprise! Dirt in a garden."

Anna covered her mouth to hide a little chuckle.

Mr. Hoffman looked over at the broccoli plants. Bailey and Mackenzie had barely pulled any of them. "It's a good idea to wear an old pair of sneakers on gardening days," he said. "Simone, how did your group do today?"

"We cleared out all the tomato plants," Imani, Simone's friend, answered for Simone. She pointed to the center of the garden where the tomato plants once stood. It was completely empty. Anna was impressed. There had been a ton of tomato plants before.

"Anna?" Mr. Hoffman sighed. "How about your group?"

"We picked all the little baking pumpkins." Anna pointed to a row of small round pumpkins lined up at the edge of the Friendship Garden. "And we're almost done pulling up what's left of the zucchini."

Reed raised his hand, but blurted his question before Mr. Hoffman could call on him. "We're not picking the jack-o'-lantern pumpkins yet, right? I need to let Herbert grow until Saturday so he can be as big as possible."

"Friday is the last meeting of the Friendship Garden's fall session," Mr. Hoffman said. "We've got to get our old plants out of the ground and cover the garden with mulch to protect the soil throughout the winter. You can leave the big pumpkins for last, but you'll have to pick them on Friday. It's time to put the garden to bed."

"I can't believe garden club is over!" said Kaya.

"Just until the spring," Anna reminded her. "Right, Mr. Hoffman?"

Instead of answering Anna's question, Mr. Hoffman tugged at his bow tie. He always wore a bow tie to school. Today's tie was orange with tiny black bats all over it. Behind her, Anna heard whispering.

"I hope my mom doesn't make me come to garden club in the spring," said Mackenzie. "This is *so* boring."

"Yeah," Bailey agreed, groaning. "So boring."

"My mom only made me come because of *your* mom," Mackenzie added. "Jamie said I should have told my mom no way like she did."

Anna turned around and looked at Bailey and Mackenzie. Along with the girl named Jamie, Bailey and Mackenzie were part of a group that Anna had nicknamed the Outfit-Outfit, because *outfit* is another word for group, and the three girls seemed to care a lot about their clothes. What they didn't seem to care about was gardening, or being nice to anyone at the Friendship Garden. Anna tried to avoid them whenever they came to meetings, just like Mr. Hoffman was trying to avoid her question.

"Mr. Hoffman?" Anna said quietly. "What will happen in the spring?"

"Well, hopefully the Friendship Garden will continue," Mr. Hoffman said. "It's just that all the Shoots and Leaves garden members have to pay money to garden here. Maria didn't make us do that this fall because we were taking over an abandoned plot that had already been paid for. But she can't allow us to garden for free in the spring, and I don't know if the school has enough money to pay the fee."

Suddenly goose bumps dotted Anna's arms. "What happens if we can't pay?"

"Don't worry!" announced Reed. "When

I win biggest pumpkin, we'll have plenty of money. First prize is one hundred dollars."

Mr. Hoffman nodded. "I hope that happens, but if we continue gardening here, we'll also need to buy our own tools. We can't keep borrowing from the other garden members. Some of them have been complaining that we haven't been taking care of their equipment. Rakes, hoes, and other tools have been left out instead of being put away in the shed. And sometimes they've been put away dirty. Having money won't matter if the other garden members don't want us here."

Anna felt her neck grow warm. She didn't like the idea of the other gardeners being mad at the Friendship Garden. It had taken Anna, Kaya, and Reed so long to persuade Maria to let them have a garden in the first place.

"All right, everyone." Mr. Hoffman stood up. "Parents will be here soon. Let's put everything away!"

Anna picked up her trowel and began to walk over to the hose. On the way, she saw Mackenzie stick muddy tools into the supply shed before she and Bailey headed to the front gate.

"Hey!" Anna chased after them. Even though she usually tried to avoid Mackenzie and Bailey, the Friendship Garden meant too much to her. "Don't forget to clean your tools!"

Bailey started to walk back to the shed, but Mackenzie rolled her eyes. "They're just going to get dirty again tomorrow. Who cares if people complain?"

Bailey stopped, then turned and looked at Anna. "Yeah," she said. "Who cares?"

"I care," said Anna. "I don't want Maria to

be sorry she let us have our own garden."

Mackenzie shrugged. "I'm already sorry she let you have it."

Bailey nodded. "I'd do *anything* for it to get canceled."

Anna couldn't believe what they were saying. Maybe *they* didn't want to come to the Friendship Garden, but why would they want to ruin it for everyone else?

Anna left Bailey and Mackenzie by the gate and got their dirty tools from the shed. Then she joined Kaya and Reed by the utility sink and washed them all.

"Herbert better win," she told Reed. "I really want to keep gardening, and we need our own tools!"

Reed nodded his head seriously. "He's going to! I already told my parents. They are finally going to see *me* win a trophy for a change instead of my brother, Dylan."

Kaya pumped her fist in the air. "You go, Reed!"

Anna looked over at Bailey and Mackenzie waiting for their parents to pick them up. Mackenzie was peering through the gate like a prisoner in a jail cell, but Bailey was staring back at the Friendship Garden. Anna guessed she was thinking mean thoughts.

So Anna tried to think some nice thoughts. She imagined the biggest pumpkin contest, and Reed holding up a giant trophy and one hundred dollars. She pictured it so strongly, she could feel the excitement and happiness swelling in her chest. Herbert just *had* to win!